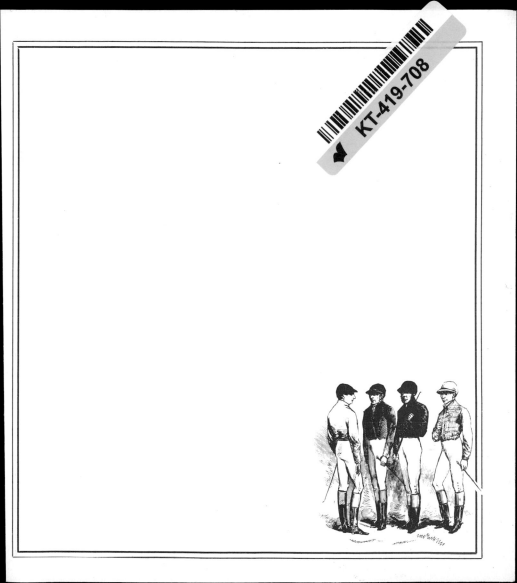

RACING
RHYMES

RACING
RHYMES

EDITED BY

P.J.M.

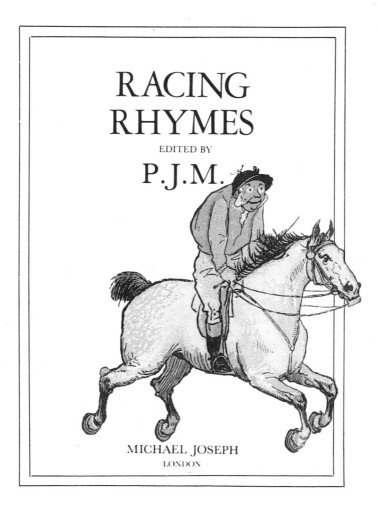

MICHAEL JOSEPH

LONDON

To
H.J. Telford
and
G.H. Mills

First published in Great Britain by
Michael Joseph Limited
27 Wrights Lane, Kensington W8
1986

British Library Cataloguing in Publication Data

Racing rhymes.
  1. Horses-racing — Anecdotes,
facetiae, satire, etc.
I. P.J.M.
798.4′00207   SF335.5

ISBN 0-7181-2778-1

Typesetting by Alacrity Phototypesetters,
Banwell Castle, Weston-super-Mare
Printed and bound in Italy

Contents

THE DERBY FOR 1840

We're off to the races,
With smiles on our faces,
Lobster salad, and champagne, and chat;
Prime Newcastle salmon,
And Westphalia "gammon;"
But there's no mistake about that.

All the world and his mother,
Are jostling each other;
City madams are "cutting it fat,"
In silks with their spouses,
In white hats and "blouses;"
There's no mistake about that.

Now, the Downs spread before us,
Sweet saints! what a chorus;
"Dorling's cards," "roulette," "All round my hat,"
Brave soldiers and seamen,
Bold thimble and pea-men;
There *is* no mistake about that.

Miscellaneous "bull-riders,"
Bestride the "outsiders,"
While of those who know what they are at,
There's Scott the *élite*,
And Robinson's seat,
There's no mistake about that.

Hark! the cry is "they've started;"
O'er the hill they have darted —
They rush round the turn for the flat;
"That's Melody leading,"
"And Scott is *succeeding* ——"
There is *some* mistake about that.

Now if Fortune was in her
Kind mood, and a winner;
You come off — don't book the thing pat —
Only, if the men "stump up,"
Why *then* you may jump up;
For there *is* no mistake about that.

CRAVEN

STEEPLECHASERS

Tucked away in winter quarters,
Gainsborough's sons and Buchan's daughters,
Blue of blood, clean-lined and handsome,
Priced beyond a prince's ransom,
Where no danger can befall them
Rest till next year's Classics call them;
And the limber lean-of-head ones,
Hardy, hefty, humble-bred ones,
Booted, bandaged to the knee,
Ready for whate'er may be,
Gallant slaves and cheery martyrs,
Stand once more before the starters.

Piggotts, Masons, Leaders, Dullers
Witch the world in mud-splashed colours,
Brushing through the birchwood switches,
Cramming at the open ditches,
Grinning when the guard-rails rattle
In the fore-front of the battle.
Gordons, Anthonys and Reeses
Bow their heads against the breezes,
Hail upon their faces whipping,
Wet reins through their fingers slipping
As they drive their 'chasers crashing
Through the fence-tops, irons clashing.

So they forge through wind and weather
To the creak of straining leather
Lashing at the leaps together,
With the fluttering flags to guide them,
Taking what the Fates provide them,
Danger calling, Death beside them.—
'Tis a game beyond gainsaying
Made by gods for brave men's playing.

WILL H. OGILVIE

The Gallant and Sprited Race
For 500gs. and 1000gs. bye — 4 miles — between

THE LATE COL. THORNTON'S LADY AND MR. FLINT.

THE ANNALS of the Turf do not contain such another extraordinary circumstance as the above match; indeed, it stands *alone* in the Sporting World, not only as a most singular contest, but as a lasting monument of FEMALE INTREPIDITY. Mrs. Thornton, it should seem, was as much attached to the Sports of the Field, as her husband, the late Colonel Thornton; she had also a great passion for horse exercise, and would try her skill and nerve in racing. The families of the Colonel and Mr. Flint lived upon terms of the greatest intimacy, the two ladies being sisters.— During one of their equestrian excursions in Thornville park, a conversation took place respecting the speed of their respective horses between Mr. Flint and Mrs. Thornton. Some difference of opinion having occurred upon the subject, the horses were put at full speed for the purpose of ascertaining the point in question, and Old *Vingarillo*, aided by the skill of the fair rider, distanced his antagonist every time, which so discomfited Mr. Flint, that he was at length induced to challenge the lady to ride on a future day. His challenge was readily accepted (on the part of the lady) by Colonel Thornton, and it was agreed that the race should take place on the last day of the York August Meeting, 1804.

On Saturday, August 25, the above match was decided in the presence of upwards of 100,000 persons. About four o'clock, Mrs. Thornton appeared on the ground in high spirits, *Old Vingarillo* led by Colonel Thornton, followed by Mr. Baker and Mr. H. Baynton, and soon afterwards Mr. Flint. Every thing being in readiness, Mrs. Thornton started amidst the loudest cheers ever heard upon a race course; and the betting all over the ground created a great deal of mirth and witty remarks from the spectators. She mounted her horse in the true spirit of a cavalier; and there was a great deal of the gallant-bearing attached to the character of it; the most experienced jockey could not have been more at his ease, or have acted his part in better style than Mrs. Thornton.

It is impossible to describe the intense interest which this match excited during the race; and the shouts of the "PETTICOAT FOR EVER," resounded from one end of the course to the other. On starting, it was 5 and 6 to 4 on the PETTICOAT; and, in running the first three miles, 7 to 4 and 2 to 1 on Mrs. Thornton's winning; indeed, success seemed to be so certain on her part, that the oldest sportsman in the stand betted in her favour. In running the last mile she lost ground, in consequence of her saddle-girths having slackened, and the saddle turning round. Her opponent, taking advantage of this circumstance, pushed forward and passed her; the lady after using every exertion but finding it impossible to win, she pulled up at two distances from home, when Mr. Flint won the match.

It was difficult to say, whether her *horsemanship*, her dress, or her beauty, were most admired, the *tout ensemble* was unique. Never, surely, did a woman ride in better style. The race was run in *nine minutes* and *fifty-nine* seconds. The dress of Mrs. Thornton was a leopard-coloured body with blue sleeves, the vest buff, and blue cap. Mr. Flint rode in white. Thus ended the most interesting race ever run upon Knavesmire.

REACTION TO THE RACE

* We cannot for a moment entertain an opinion, that the ladies meant any thing *unfair* in the conduct pursued by Mr. Flint during the race towards Mrs. Thornton; neither did they assert that any thing like *crossing*, or *jostling*, occurred in the four miles; but that as a man of *gallantry*, he ought to have permitted his fair opponent to have won the race. But, perhaps, Mr. Flint would have felt rather chagrined to have had the *laugh* against him; and also averse to the observation that he had been "beaten against his will, on horseback, by a woman;" which, most undoubtedly, would have been the fact, if the saddle of Mrs. Thornton had kept its situation.

PIERCE EGAN'S BOOK OF SPORTS

NEWMARKET

ARRIVING AT *Newmarket* in the Month of *October*, I had the Opportunity to see the Horse-Races; and a great Concourse of the Nobility and Gentry, as well from *London* as from all Parts of *England*; but they were all so intent, so eager, so busy upon their Wagers and Bets, that to me they seemed just like so many Horse-coursers in *Smithfield*, descending from their high Dignity and Quality, to picking one another's Pockets, and biting one another as much as possible; and that with such Eagerness, as it might be said they acted without respect to Faith, Honour, or good Manners.

DANIEL DEFOE

LORD HIPPO

Lord Hippo suffered fearful loss
By putting money on a horse
Which he believed, if it were pressed,
Would run far faster than the rest:
For Someone who was in the know
Had confidently told him so.
But on the morning of the race
It only took the *seventh* place!

Picture the Viscount's great surprise!
He scarcely could believe his eyes!
He sought the Individual who
Had laid him odds at 9 to 2,
Suggesting as a useful tip
That they should enter Partnership
And put to joint account the debt
Arising from his foolish bet.
But when the Bookie — oh! my word,
I only wish you could have heard
The way he roared he did not think,
And hoped that they might strike him pink!
Lord Hippo simply turned and ran
From this infuriated man.
Despairing, maddened, and distraught
He utterly collapsed and sought
His Sire, the Earl of Potamus,
And brokenly addressed him thus:
"Dread Sire — to-day — at Ascot — I..."
His genial parent made reply:
"Come! Come! Come! Come! don't look so glum!
Trust your Papa and name the sum ...
... Fifteen hundred thousand? ... Hum!
However ... stiffen up, you wreck;
Boys will be boys — so here's the cheque!"
Lord Hippo, feeling deeply — well,
More grateful than he dared to tell —
Punted the lot on Little Nell: —
And got a telegram at dinner
To say that he had backed the Winner!

HILAIRE BELLOC

THE START. — THEY'RE OFF

They're off! they're off! the shout, the cry,
  Extend along the plain;
And countless hearts are beating high,
  And countless eyeballs strain!

Rebounding and resounding hoofs
  Are heard afar — now near!
Yes, here they are! the gallant steeds
  Swift as the wind appear.

ANON.

NATIONAL VELVET

AT THE POST the twenty horses were swaying like the sea. Forward . . .
. . . No good! Back again. Forward . . . No good! Back again.

The line formed . . . and rebroke. Waves of the sea. Drawing a breath
. . . breaking. Velvet fifth from the rail, between a bay and a brown. The
Starter had long finished his instructions. Nothing more was said aloud,
but low oaths flew, the cursing and grumbling flashed like a storm. An
eye glanced at her with a look of hate. The breaking of movement was
too close to movement to be borne. It was like water clinging to the tilted
rim of the glass, like the sound of the dreaded explosion after the great
shell has fallen. The will to surge forward overlaid by something delicate

and terrible and strong, human obedience at bursting-point, but not broken. Horses' eyes gleamed openly, men's eyes set like chips of steel. Rough man, checked in violence, barely master of himself, barely master of his horse. The Piebald ominously quiet, and nothing coming from him ... up went the tape.

The green Course poured in a river before her as she lay forward, and with the plunge of movement sat in the stream.

"Black slugs ..." said Mi, cursing under his breath, running, dodging, suffocated with the crowd. It was the one thing he had overlooked, that the crowd was too dense to allow him to reach Becher's in the time. "God's liver," he mumbled, his throat gone cold, and stumbled into an old fool in a mackintosh. "Are they off?" he yelled at the heavy crowd as he ran, but no one bothered with him. He was cursed if he was heeded at all. He ran, gauging his position by the cranes on the embankment. Velvet coming over Becher's in a minute and he not there to see her. "They're off!" All around him a sea of throats offered up the gasp.

He was opposite Becher's but could see nothing: the crowd thirty deep between him and the Course. All around fell the terrible silence of expectancy. Mi stood like a rock. If he could not see then he must use his ears, hear. Enclosed in the dense, silent, dripping pack he heard the thunder coming. It roared up on the wet turf like the single approach of a multiple-footed animal. There were stifled exclamations, grunts, thuds. Something in the air flashed and descended. The first over Becher's! A roar went up from the crowd, then silence. The things flashing in the air were indistinguishable. The tip of a cap exposed for the briefest of seconds. The race went by like an express train, and was gone. Could Velvet be alive in that?

ENID BAGNOLD

[19]

RIGHT ROYAL

In a race-course box behind the Stand
Right Royal shone from a strapper's hand.
A big dark bay with a restless tread,
Fetlock deep in a wheat-straw bed;
A noble horse of a nervy blood,
By O Mon Roi out of Rectitude.
Something quick in his eye and ear
Gave a hint that he might be queer.
In front, he was all to a horseman's mind;
Some thought him a trifle light behind.
By two good points might his rank be known,
A beautiful head and a Jumping Bone.

He had been the hope of Sir Button Budd,
Who bred him there at the Fletchings stud,
But the Fletchings jockey had flogged him cold
In a narrow thing as a two-year-old.
After that, with his sulks and swerves,
Dread of the crowd and fits of nerves,
Like a wastrel bee who makes no honey,
He had hardly earned his entry money.

Liking him still, though he failed at racing,
Sir Button trained him for steeple-chasing.
He jumped like a stag, but his heart was cowed;
Nothing would make him face the crowd.
When he reached the Straight where the crowds began
He would make no effort for any man.
Sir Button sold him, Charles Cothill bought him,
Rode him to hounds and soothed and taught him.
After two years' care Charles felt assured
That his horse's broken heart was cured,
And the jangled nerves in tune again.

And now, as proud as a King of Spain,
He moved in his box with a restless tread,
His eyes like sparks in his lovely head,
Ready to run between the roar
Of the stands that face the Straight once more;
Ready to race, though blown, though beat,
As long as his will could lift his feet;
Ready to burst his heart to pass
Each gasping horse in that street of grass.

JOHN MASEFIELD

THE BOY IN YELLOW

When first I strove to win the prize,
I felt my youthful spirits rise;
Hope's crimson flush illum'd my face,
And all my soul was in the race.
When weigh'd and mounted, 'twas my pride,
Before the starting post to ride;
My rival's drest in red and green,
But I in simple yellow seen.

In stands around fair ladies swarm,
And mark with smiles my slender form;
Their lovely looks new ardour raise,
For beauty's smile is merit's praise!
The flag is dropt — the sign to start —
Away more fleet than winds we dart,
And tho' the odds against me lay,
The boy in yellow wins the day!

Tho' now no more we seek the race,
I trust the jockey keeps his place;
For still to win the prize, I feel
An equal wish, an equal zeal:
And still can beauty's smile impart
Delightful tremors thro' this heart:
Indeed, I feel it flutter now —
Yes, while I look, and while I bow!

My tender years must vouch my truth —
For candor ever dwells with youth;
Then sure the sage might well believe,
A face — like mine — could ne'er deceive,
If here you o'er a match should make,
My life upon my luck I'll stake;
And 'gainst all odds, I think you'll say,
The boy in yellow wins the day.

SONGS OF THE CHACE

UPPER LAMBOURNE

Up the ash-tree climbs the ivy,
  Up the ivy climbs the sun,
With a twenty-thousand pattering
  Has a valley breeze begun,
Feathery ash, neglected elder,
  Shift the shade and make it run —

Shift the shade toward the nettles,
   And the nettles set it free
To streak the stained Carrara headstone
   Where, in nineteen-twenty-three,
He who trained a hundred winners
   Paid the Final Entrance Fee.

Leathery limbs of Upper Lambourne,
   Leathery skin from sun and wind,
Leathery breeches, spreading stables,
   Shining saddles left behind—
To the down the string of horses
   Moving out of sight and mind.

Feathery ash in leathery Lambourne
   Waves above the sarsen stone,
And Edwardian plantations
   So coniferously moan
As to make the swelling downland,
   Far-surrounding, seem their own.

JOHN BETJEMAN

A HORSE UP-STAIRS

IN THE YEAR 1851, at one of the early meetings of the Aylesbury Aristo-cratic Steeplechases, and during the stewards' dinner at the White Hart in the grand old Rochester Room, the following event occurred.

The conversation turned to the fact that the Marquis of Waterford had once taken a noted hunter up the stairs and led him round the dining-table in this very room, whilst the noble Master of the Buck-hounds, the Earl of Erroll, and his guests fed the horse on biscuits and apples. One of the young Oxford gentlemen, well known for his splendid riding, said, "I believe the little grey would come up these or any other stairs." It was asked if the trial might be made, and down went two or three choice spirits into the stable-yard, and, to the astonishment of the party (nearly fifty people being present) a lumbering noise was heard on the stairs, and presently in walked the gallant grey. After leading him round the table and resting him before a large fire which blazed in the fine old grate before which many a time and oft poor Nellie Gwynne had warmed her dainty feet, the horse, led by a halter, was induced to jump over the backs of a couple of chairs. Then, J. Leech Manning, a sporting farmer of the neighbourhood, said he would undertake to ride him over the dinner-table (it should be mentioned that the dinner was still in progress, the third course was being consumed, the decanters of wine going their round, the candelabra all alight, and various wax lights as well were sparkling on the board). No sooner said than Manning jumped on to the barebacked horse, and taking the halter in his hand, he rode him up into the corner of the room, which was about forty feet long by twenty-two feet wide: Manning struck the horse with his heel, and with a slap on his neck with his right hand he sent him flying over the table, covered as it was with all the usual appurtenances to a repast: he cleared it well, then, to the surprise of all, he turned the horse in splendid style and jumped him back again.

J.K. Fowler

ONLY A JOCKEY

Out in the grey cheerless chill of the morning light,
　Out on the track where the night shades still lurk;
Ere the first gleam of the sungod's returning light,
　Round come the race-horses early at work.

Reefing and pulling and racing so readily,
　Close sit the jockey-boys holding them hard,
"Steady the stallion there — canter him steadily,
　"Don't let him gallop so much as a yard."

Fiercely he fights while the others run wide of him,
　Reefs at the bit that would hold him in thrall,
Plunges and bucks till the boy that's astride of him
　Goes to the ground with a terrible fall.

"Stop him there! Block him there! Drive him in carefully,
　"Lead him about till he's quiet and cool.
"Sound as a bell! though he's blown himself fearfully,
　"Now let us pick up this poor little fool.

"Stunned? Oh, by Jove, I'm afraid it's a case with him;
　"Ride for the doctor! keep bathing his head!
Send for a cart to go down to our place with him" —
　No use! One long sigh and the little chap's dead.

Only a jockey-boy, foul-mouthed and bad you see,
　Ignorant, heathenish, gone to his rest.
Parson or Presbyter, Pharisee, Sadducee,
　What did you do for him? — bad was the best.

Negroes and foreigners, all have a claim on you;
　　Yearly you send your well-advertised hoard,
But the poor jockey-boy — shame on you, shame on you,
　　"Feed ye, my little ones" — what said the Lord?

Him ye held less than the outer barbarian,
　　Left him to die in his ignorant sin;
Have you no principles, humanitarian?
　　Have you no precept — "go gather them in?"

　　　　．　　．　　．　　．　　．　　．

Knew he God's name? In his brutal profanity,
　　That name was an oath — out of many but one —
What did he get from our famed Christianity?
　　Where has his soul — if he had any — gone?

Fourteen years old, and what was he taught of it?
　　What did he know of God's infinite grace?
Draw the dark curtain of shame o'er the thought of it,
　　Draw the shroud over the jockey-boy's face.

A. B. PATERSON

KING WILLIAM AT ASCOT

THE RIDE through the great park, the appearance of the noble trees, the beautiful surrounding picturesque scenery, the dashing charioteers along the road, the venerable castle, enriching, and giving the prospect a perfect climax, altogether make the journey to Ascot races one of the most desirable places for a week's pleasure in the kingdom. His present majesty, king William, has not been so much interested on the turf as his royal brother, the late king George, and his royal highness, the duke of York. But, nevertheless, his present Majesty enters into all the spirit of the lively scene, and appears to enjoy it equal to any of the sporting characters present. During the last races, after the king was asked how many of his horses should start for a certain plate, his majesty answered, with great *naïvete*,

"O let all the FLEET run!"

PIERCE EGAN'S
BOOK OF SPORTS

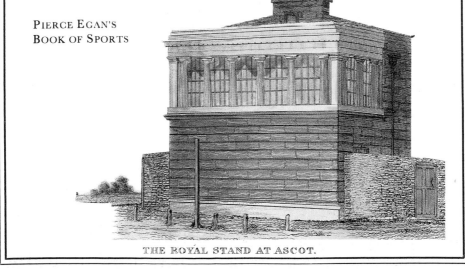

THE ROYAL STAND AT ASCOT.

LORRAINE, LORRAINE, LORRÉE

Are you ready for your steeplechase, Lorraine, Lorraine, Lorrée?
  Barum, Barum, Barum, Barum, Barum, Barum, Baree,
You're booked to ride your capping race to-day at Coulterlee,
You're booked to ride Vindictive, for all the world to see,
To keep him straight, to keep him first, and win the race for me.
  Barum, Barum, &c.

She clasped her new-born baby, poor Lorraine, Lorraine, Lorrée.
"I cannot ride Vindictive as any man might see,
And I will not ride Vindictive, with this baby on my knee;
He's killed a boy, he's killed a man, and why must he kill me?"

"Unless you ride Vindictive, Lorraine, Lorraine, Lorrée,
Unless you ride Vindictive to-day at Coulterlee,
And land him safe across the brook, and win the blank for me,
It's you may keep your baby, for you'll get no keep from me."

"That husbands could be cruel," said Lorraine, Lorraine, Lorrée,
"That husbands could be cruel, I have known for seasons three;
But oh! to ride Vindictive while a baby cries for me,
And be killed across a fence at last for all the world to see!"

She mastered young Vindictive — oh! the gallant lass was she —
And kept him straight and won the race as near as near could be;
But he killed her at the brook against a pollard willow tree,
Oh! he killed her at the brook, the brute, for all the world to see,
And no one but the baby cried for poor Lorraine, Lorrée.

CHARLES KINGSLEY

BOOKEY

I went toward the Members' stand, my patrons to be near,
The keeper at the gate, sez he, "We want no Bookeys here;"
The swells a-passin' through they grinned and sniggered fit to die;
I paid the sum for Tattersall's, and to myself sez I:
   O it's Bookey this, and Bookey that, and "Bookey, go away;
   We're far too swell to have you near, so by the railings stay;
   Behind the railings is your place, so please behind them stay,
   And when we want you we will come." So there I had to stay.

I looked above the iron rails, as patient as could be,
Is cheaper far than honour — and with some that's deucèd cheap;
We are not fit to mix with them — our calling's far too low —
But if we stopped away, I guess, they'd find it precious slow.
   For it's Bookey this, and Bookey that, and "Bookey, keep away;"
   But there's safety in the Bookey when the time comes round to pay;
   When the time comes round to pay, my lords, the time comes round to pay;
   You feel safest with the Bookeys when the time comes round to pay.

Yes, making mock of those you use, and for your pleasure keep,
Is cheaper far than honour — and with some that's ducèd cheap;
And betting with a Bookey, on a certain tip you've got,
Is safer far than it would be with some of your own lot.
   Then it's Bookey this, and Bookey that, and "Bookey, don't come near;"
   But it's "Where's my good friend Dickey Jones?" when the numbers do
     appear;
   When the numbers do appear at last, the numbers do appear;
   O it's "Where's my best of Bookeys?" when the numbers do appear.

We ain't all whitewashed angels, nor we ain't all blacklegs, too,
But men as fancies betting, most remarkable like you;
And if you find our language not always to your mind,
A-bawling odds through railings don't make voices too refined.

While it's Bookey this, and Bookey that, and "Bookey, fall behind:"
But they come and look us up at times, when tips are in the wind;
When tips are in the wind, my boys, when tips are in the wind;
They come upon the strict q.t. when tips are in the wind.

They talk about reforming us, but, if they wish to try,
They'd better sweep the top-floor first, for dirt will downward fly.
It's little use our clearing up before they make a start,
For we shall always be, as now, their lower counterpart.
  For it's Blackleg this, and Blackleg that, and "Chuck him out, the cad!"
  If we, like other folks get broke, or trot off to the bad;
  And it's Bookey this, and Bookey that, and treat him as you please;
  But Bookey ain't a blooming ass — you bet that Bookey sees.

S. F. OUTWOOD

from
MAIDEN STAKES

GIVEN A summer's day, Royal Ascot may be almost too good to be true. If it were a play, the stage-management would be hailed a miracle. But it is not a play. It is an English festival, kept by the English and their friends, with the King and Queen of England keeping it in their midst. More. It is a high festival. His Majesty is in his State.

The beauty of the course and its surroundings, the rich green of the turf, the sparkle of the clean, white paintwork, the sharp shadows flung by the stands make up a setting which only some shining function could ever fill: the flowers, the fine green liveries of the servants, the brave show and promise of the Royal Box, above all, the air of expectation deck and furnish that setting to a degree of quality very seldom met with in this workaday world: and the ceaseless movement of thousands, eager, care-free, yet full-dressed and on parade, renders a Court of Honour fit for a King.

Shortly before the first race, far down the course, a glittering streak upon the green argues a cavalcade.

Very slowly the Procession takes shape.

Scarlet and gold and velvet, wigs and cockades, postilions and out-riders, and the magnificent greys, down the midst of the broad, green lane at a royal pace come the King's horses and the King's men. And the King and his Queen in their carriage, with the Equerries riding beside and their Train behind. Match me that quiet progress, match me that sight in the sunshine, match me the brilliance of that moment — Tradition itself ennobled by the unceremonious perfection with which it is observed.

Then the Royal Standard is broken, and the festival is begun.

DORNFORD YATES

THE HIGH-METTLED RACER

See the course throng'd with gazers, the sports are begun,
Confusion but hear, I bet you sir, done:
Ten thousand strange murmurs resound far and near,
Lords, hawkers, and jockies, assail the tir'd ear;
While with neck like a rainbow erecting his crest,
Pamper'd, prancing, and pleas'd, his head touching his breast,
Scarcely snuffing the air, he's so proud and elate,
The high-mettled Racer first starts for the plate.

Now Reynard's turn'd out, and o'er hedge and ditch rush,
Dogs, horses, and huntsmen, all hard at his brush;
Thro' marsh, fen, and brier, led by their sly prey,
They by scent, and by view, chace a long tedious way;
While alike born for sports of the field and the course,
Always sure to come through — a stanch and fleet horse;
When fairly run down, the Fox yields up his breath,
The high-mettled Racer is in at the death.

Grown aged, us'd up, and turn'd out of the stud,
Lame, spavin'd, and wind-gall'd, but yet with some blood,
While knowing postillions his pedigree trace,
Tell his dame won this sweep, his sire won that race,
And what matches he won to the hostlers count o'er,
As they loiter their time at some hedge-ale-house door,
While the harness sore galls, and the spurs his sides goad,
The high-mettled Racer's a hack on the road.

Till at last having labour'd, dragg'd early and late,
Bow'd down by degrees he bends on to his fate,
Blind, old, lean, and feeble, he tugs round a mill,
Or draws sand, till the sand of his hourglass stands still;
And now cold and lifeless, expos'd to the view,
In the very same cart that he yesterday drew,
While a pitying crowd his sad relics surrounds,
The high-mettled Racer is sold for the hounds.

ANON.

HOW WE BEAT THE FAVOURITE

(A Lay of the Loamshire Hunt Cup)

"Aye, squire," said Stevens, "they back him at evens!
   The race is all over, bar shouting, they say;
The Clown ought to beat her; Dick Neville is sweeter
   Than ever — he swears he can win all the way.

"A gentleman rider — well, I'm an outsider,
   But if he's a gent, who the mischief's a jock?
Your swells mostly blunder, Dick rides for the plunder,
   He rides, too, like thunder — he sits like a rock.

Some parting injunction, bestowed with great unction,
  I tried to recall, but forgot like a dunce,
When Reginald Murray, full tilt on White Surrey,
  Came down in a hurry to start us at once.

"Keep back in the yellow! Come up on Othello!
  Hold hard on the chestnut! Turn round on the Drag!
Keep back there on Spartan! Back you, sir, in tartan!
  So, steady there, easy," and down went the flag.

She passed like an arrow Kildare and Cock-Sparrow,
  And Mantrap and Mermaid refused the stone wall;
And Giles on the Greyling came down at the paling,
  And I was left sailing in front of them all.

I took them a burster, nor eased her nor nursed her
  Until the Black Bullfinch led into the plough,
And through the strong bramble we bored with a scramble,
  My cap was knocked off by the hazel-tree bough.

She rose when I hit her. I saw the stream glitter,
  A wide scarlet nostril flashed close to my knee,
Between sky and water the Clown came and caught her,
  The space that he cleared was a caution to see.

She raced at the rasper, I felt my knees grasp her,
  I found my hands give to her strain on the bit,
She rose when the Clown did — our silks as we bounded
  Brush'd lightly, our stirrups clash'd loud as we lit.

A rise steeply sloping, a fence with stone coping, —
The last — we diverged round the base of the hill;
His path was the nearer, his leap was the clearer,
  I flogg'd up the straight, and he led sitting still.

On still past the gateway she strains in the straight-way,
  Still struggles, "The Clown by a short neck at most!"
He swerves, the green scourges, the stand rocks and surges,
  And flashes, and verges, and flits the white post.

Aye! so ends the tussle — I knew the tan muzzle
  Was first, though the ring-men were yelling "Dead-heat!"
A nose I could swear by, but Clarke said "The mare by
  A short head!" And that's how the favourite was beat.

Adam Lindsay Gordon

THE PRINCE REGENT AT BRIGHTON

"In those days, the Prince made Brighton and Lewes Races the gayest scene of the year in England. The Pavilion was full of guests, and the Steyne was crowded with all the rank and fashion from London. About half an hour before the departure for the hill, the Prince himself would make his appearance in the crowd. I think I see him now, in a green jacket, a white hat, and light nankeen pantaloons and shoes, distinguished by his high-bred manner and handsome person. The Downs were soon covered with every species of conveyance, and the Prince's German waggon and six bay horses (so were barouches called when first introduced at that time) issued out of the gates of the Pavilion, and, gliding up the green ascent, was stationed close to the Grand Stand, where it remained the centre of attraction for the day. At dinner-time the Pavilion was resplendent with lights, and a sumptuous banquet was furnished to a large party; while those who were not included in that invitation found a dinner, with every luxury, at the Club-house on the Steyne."   Raike's Diary

AT GRASS

The eye can hardly pick them out
From the cold shade they shelter in,
Till wind distresses tail and mane;
Then one crops grass, and moves about
— The other seeming to look on —
And stands anonymous again.

Yet fifteen years ago, perhaps
Two dozen distances sufficed
To fable them: faint afternoons
Of Cups and Stakes and Handicaps,
Whereby their names were artificed
To inlay faded, classic Junes —

Silks at the start: against the sky
Numbers and parasols: outside,
Squadrons of empty cars, and heat,
And littered grass: then the long cry
Hanging unhushed till it subside
To stop-press columns on the street.

Do memories plague their ears like flies?
They shake their heads. Dusk brims the shadows.
Summer by summer all stole away,
The starting-gates, the crowds and cries —
All but the unmolesting meadows.
Almanacked, their names live; they

Have slipped their names, and stand at ease,
Or gallop for what must be joy,
And not a fieldglass sees them home,
Or curious stop-watch prophesies:
Only the groom, and the groom's boy,
With bridles in the evening come.

PHILIP LARKIN

THE HOOFS OF THE HORSES

The hoofs of the horses! — Oh! witching and sweet
Is the music earth steels from the iron-shod feet;
No whisper of lover, no trilling of bird
Can stir me as hoofs of the horses have stirred.

They spurn disappointment and trample despair,
And drown with their drum-beats the challenge of care;
With scarlet and silk for their banners above,
They are swifter than Fortune and sweeter than Love.

On the wings of the morning they gather and fly,
In the hush of the night-time I hear them go by —
The horses of memory thundering through
With flashing white fetlocks all wet with the dew.

When you lay me to slumber no spot you can choose
But will ring to the rhythm of galloping shoes,
And under the daisies no grave be so deep
But the hoofs of the horses shall sound in my sleep.

WILL H. OGILVIE

ACKNOWLEDGEMENTS

I am greatly indebted to Mr. Owen Rees without whose unfailing wit, good humour and encouragement, this book would not now appear in its present form.

The editor and publishers would like to thank the following for permission to quote: Gerald Duckworth & Co Limited for 'Lord Hippo' by Hilaire Belloc (from *More Peers*); The Heinemann Group of Publishers for the extract from *National Velvet* by Enid Bagnold; The Society of Authors and the Literary representative of the estate of John Masefield for the verses from *Right Royal*; John Murray (Publishers) Ltd for 'Upper Lambourne' from *Collected Poems* of Sir John Betjeman; Ward Locke for the extract from *Maiden Stakes* by Dornford Yates and Marvell Press for 'At Grass' from *The Less Deceived* by Philip Larkin.

The illustrations on pages 9 and 13 appear by courtesy of The Radio Times Hulton Picture Library; those on pages 19, 29, 37, 39 and 43 by the Mary Evans Picture Library; those on pages 21, 25, 33, and 45 by the Bridgeman Arts Library and that on page 14 by the proprietors of Punch.

I have been unable to trace the owners of certain copyrights and beg the forgiveness of anyone whose rights have been overlooked.